D1132996

Weekly Reader Children's Book Club presents

This is a registered trademark

GUS AND THE BABY GHOST

By JANE THAYER

PICTURES BY SEYMOUR FLEISHMAN

William Morrow and Company
New York 1972

Text copyright © 1972 by Catherine Woolley
Illustrations copyright © 1972 by Seymour Fleishman
All rights reserved. No part of this book may be reproduced
or utilized in any form or by any means, electronic or mechanical,
including photocopying, recording or by any information storage
and retrieval system, without permission in writing
from the Publisher. Inquiries should be addressed to
William Morrow and Company,
Inc., 105 Madison Ave., New York, N.Y. 10016.
Printed in the United States of America.
Library of Congress Catalog Card Number 76-161874
Weekly Reader Children's Book Club Edition

Gus the ghost and Mr. Frizzle
ran the Historical Museum,
Gus at night, Mr. Frizzle during the day.
Mr. Frizzle lived upstairs;
Gus had an attic apartment.
Cora the cat lived here and there,
and Mouse the mouse
had his own private quarters.
Late one night,
when Gus
was in charge,
Cora came in
from a moonlight walk,
and said,
"A baby ghost's outside."

Sure enough,
a baby ghost
wrapped in
a ghostly blanket
lay on the step.

"What do I do with it?" Gus cried.
"Waa!" yelled the baby ghost.
"Feed," said Cora.
Grown-up ghosts never get hungry,
but baby ghosts often do.

Gus carried the baby ghost in its blanket
into the old-fashioned kitchen
and found some milk.
"Warm," advised Cora.
Gus warmed the milk.
"Bottle," said Cora.
Gus made some ghostly remarks,
and a baby's bottle appeared.

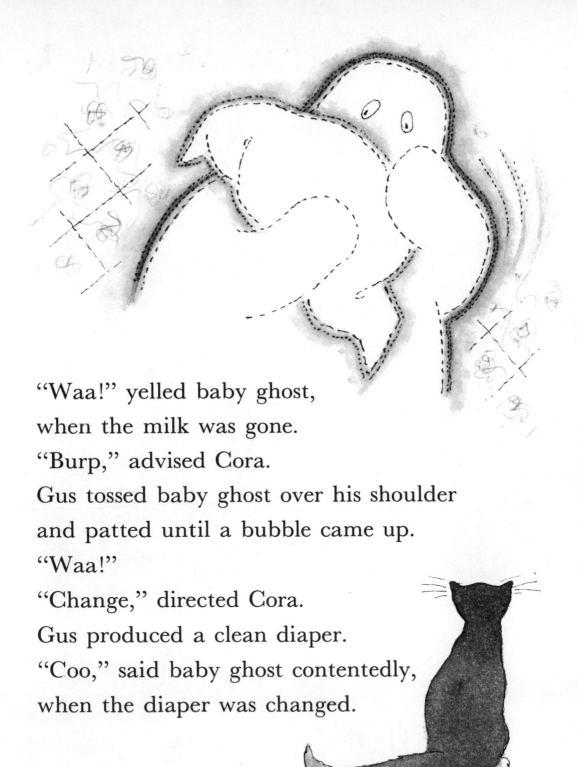

"Waa!" yelled baby ghost,
when the milk was gone.
"Burp," advised Cora.
Gus tossed baby ghost over his shoulder
and patted until a bubble came up.
"Waa!"
"Change," directed Cora.
Gus produced a clean diaper.
"Coo," said baby ghost contentedly,
when the diaper was changed.

"Sleepy," said Cora.
Gus had just laid baby ghost
in the antique cradle
and covered it with the old paisley shawl
when Mr. Frizzle came running downstairs,
his bathrobe flying.

"I thought I heard a baby," he cried.

"Baby ghost," corrected Gus.

"Where?" yelled Mr. Frizzle.

"Cradle," said Gus.

The cradle looked empty to Frizzle,

but he could see it was rocking gently.

"What in thunder

is it doing here?" he shouted.

"Sleeping," said Gus.

Mr. Frizzle, who had a terrible temper,

began to shout and tell Gus

he wouldn't have a baby ghost in his museum.

Gus began to shout back,

not knowing what else to do.

Cora went under the Boston rocker,

and Mouse scurried into the wall.

Baby ghost waked up, with all this noise,
and yelled, "Waa!"
Cora yowled, "Meow!"
Mouse snarled, "Shut up!"
"Go to bed, Frizzle!" shouted Gus.

Finally Mr. Frizzle pounded upstairs.
When he had gone,
Gus sat down with a sigh of relief
in the Boston rocker,
and Cora leaped onto his lap.

Gus rocked the cradle
until baby ghost fell asleep.
Gus understood how Mr. Frizzle felt.
Frizzle was proud
that many people came to see the museum,
and he didn't want anything
to frighten them.
Gus kept out of the way,
but a crying baby ghost might not.
I'll do something tomorrow, thought Gus.
He fell asleep rocking the cradle,
baby ghost slept, and Cora slept.
Only Mouse whisked about busily,
looking for a crumb of something.

When daylight came,
Gus warmed another bottle for baby ghost.
"Bath," advised Cora.
Gus got a baby's bathtub
and filled it with warm ghostly water.
Baby ghost was so cute,
splashing and happily gurgling,
that Gus began to feel happy himself.
When he had it all dry
and smelling of ghostly talcum powder,
he decided he would like to keep
this little baby ghost.

But I can't keep it in my attic apartment,
he told himself.
It has to sleep in the cradle.
Besides, my ghostly bones
are too old to run upstairs with bottles.
He carried baby ghost
back to the old cradle.
"Waa!" cried baby ghost,
who was hungry again.
Down came Frizzle, filled with fury.
"It's still here!" he cried.
"Sh!" said Gus.

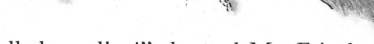

"Call the police!" shouted Mr. Frizzle.
"Very funny!" said Gus.
"Waa!" yelled baby ghost.

Mr. Frizzle called the police himself.
"There's a baby ghost
at the Historical Museum.
Come and get it."
"Beg pardon?" said the police.
"I want to get rid of a baby ghost!"
shouted Mr. Frizzle.
Two policemen came.
"What seems to be the trouble?" they said.

"We've got a baby ghost," said Mr. Frizzle.
"Are you feeling all right, Mr. Frizzle?"
asked the police.
"I feel fine!" shouted Frizzle.
"Show us this baby ghost,"
said the policemen politely.

But Gus had decided that he was going
to scare the policemen away.
He raced upstairs
and brought down his bang-clank equipment,
which he kept in case somebody wanted
to hear a ghost clanking around.

BANG, CLANK! went Gus
on his bang-clank equipment.
"Waa!" yelled baby ghost at the noise.
The policemen turned pale
and bumped into each other
rushing out the door.

Just then an early visitor arrived.
"Keep that kid quiet!" hissed Frizzle.
Gus snatched baby ghost from the cradle
and gave it a bottle.
He sang a ghostly lullaby
until it went back to sleep.

Frizzle felt calmer when the visitor left
without knowing they had a baby ghost.
He said in a reasonable voice, "Now, Gus,
you know you've got to get rid of it."
If I keep it quiet, Gus thought craftily,
Frizzle never will know it's here.
"Leave it to me, Frizzle," he said,
and Mr. Frizzle went off, reassured.
Then Gus got a book
on the care and feeding of baby ghosts.

He ordered milk from the milkman
and put in supplies of baby food,
ghostly diapers, and talcum powder,
to keep baby ghost comfy.
He found a ghostly rattle
and other toys to keep it amused.
He oiled the antique music box,
so it played tinkly tunes
that baby ghost liked to hear.
Baby ghost was content and didn't cry.

But one day Mr. Frizzle,
who thought the baby ghost was gone,
happened to be passing the cradle
when he heard a soft "Coo."
He stopped short and stared at the cradle.
"You didn't get rid of it!" he shouted.
"Waa!" yelled baby ghost,
alarmed at the noise.
"Meow!" yowled Cora, alarmed by baby ghost.
"Listen, Frizzle!" yelled Gus.

Then he lowered his voice.
"If you would control your temper,
everything would be fine!"
Finally Mr. Frizzle sat down
in the Boston rocker,
not knowing what else to do.
He lowered his voice too,
and said, "Har. Humpf."
He stared at the cradle,
which still looked empty to him.

"Do you swear it won't cry
and ruin business?" he demanded.
"If you don't come roaring around,"
retorted Gus.
"Har. Humpf," said Mr. Frizzle.
Then Gus put up a large sign,

Quiet, please

to remind Mr. Frizzle.
Mr. Frizzle began to talk
to visitors in hushed tones.
He stopped shouting at Gus.
He didn't even say, "Har, humpf,"
because he didn't want to make
baby ghost cry and alarm the people.
But Gus saw him glance
at the cradle sometimes,
and he knew Mr. Frizzle was nervous.

One day Mr. Frizzle
was telling a lady visitor in hushed tones,
so he wouldn't wake baby ghost,
"This is an antique cradle."
Suddenly Mr. Frizzle, the visitor,
and Gus, who was nearby,
were startled to hear quite plainly, "Coo!"

"Have you got a baby ghost?"
the lady cried.
"Certainly not!" cried Frizzle.
"Oh, I wish you had a baby ghost!"
said the lady sadly.
Frizzle looked at the lady in surprise.
He eyed her suspiciously.
Was she joking?
He liked to please
the visitors to his museum.
So finally Frizzle said cautiously,
"We might have a *small* baby ghost."
The lady rushed off to tell her friends
that this wonderful, delightful
Historical Museum
had something very special—
a real baby ghost!

Soon crowds of people came, tiptoed in,
and stood around waiting to hear
the baby ghost, in the antique cradle
under the old paisley shawl,
say, "Coo!"

"Your baby ghost sounds so happy,"
everyone whispered.
Mr. Frizzle proudly whispered back,
"Our baby ghost has a happy home,
that's why."

Before long baby ghost
was a permanent member of the household.
Sometimes,
when the museum closed after a busy day,
Mr. Frizzle sat down in the Boston rocker
in a rare good humor.
Cora leaped onto his lap.
Mouse kept as quiet as a mouse.
Mr. Frizzle rocked the cradle,

while Gus hung baby ghost's
ghostly washing out in the evening air.